little miss Late

by Roger Hargreaves

© Mrs Roger Hargreaves 1981
Printed and published 1993 under licence from Price Stern Sloan Inc.,
Los Angeles. All rights reserved.
Published in Great Britain by World International Publishing Limited,
An Egmont Company, Egmont House, P.O. Box 111, Great Ducie Street,
Manchester M60 3BL. Printed in Finland. ISBN 0-7498-1553-1
Reprinted 1993
A CIP catalogue record for this book is available from the British Library

Late for this.

Late for that.

Little Miss Late was late for everything!

For instance.

Do you know where she spent last Christmas?

At home.

Earlybird Cottage!

But, do you know when she spent Christmas?

January 25th!

One month late!

For example.

Do you know when she did her spring cleaning at Earlybird Cottage?

In the summer!

Three months late!

For instance.

Do you know when she went on her summer holiday last year?

In December!

Six months late!

Earlybird Cottage was just along the road from where a friend of hers lived.

Little Miss Neat.

Little Miss Neat was out for an evening stroll last October when she looked over the hedge of Earlybird Cottage.

Miss Late was in the garden.

"Hello," called out little Miss Neat. "What are you doing?"

"I thought I'd cut the grass!" replied Miss Late.

"I think," remarked little Miss Neat, looking at the grass, "that you should have thought about that last April!"

"Tell you what," suggested Miss Neat. "Let's go shopping together tomorrow!"

"Good idea," agreed Miss Late.

"I'll meet you in town on the corner of Main Street tomorrow afternoon," said Miss Neat.

"Two o'clock!"

"I'll be there," replied Miss Late.

The following afternoon little Miss Neat stood on the corner of Main Street at two o'clock.

Waiting for Miss Late.

She waited.

And waited.

And waited some more.

Miss Late arrived.

"Sorry I'm a bit late," she apologised.

"Sorry?" cried Miss Neat. "A bit late? It's five o'clock and all the shops are shut!!"

"Sorry," said Miss Late.

And that's what happened, all the time!

It happened when Miss Late decided to take a job.

Her first job was in a bank.

But the trouble was, by the time she arrived for work, the bank had closed for the day.

Every day!

"Sorry," she said.

They asked her to leave.

It happened in her second job, as a waitress in a restaurant.

Mr Greedy came in for lunch.

He glanced at the menu.

"I'll have everything," he grinned.

"Twice!"

He was still waiting to be served at seven o'clock.

So he went home.

"Sorry," said little Miss Late.

They asked her to leave.

It happened in her third job, working as a secretary for Mr Uppity.

"I'd like these letters typed before I go home," Mr Uppity said to her.
He went home at four o'clock.

In the morning!

"Sorry," said little Miss Late.

He asked her to leave.

However, as it happened, which is often the way of things, little Miss Late managed to find herself the perfect job.

She now works for Mr Lazy!

She cooks and cleans for him.

Cleaning his house every morning.

Cooking his lunch every lunchtime.

Now.

Mr Lazy, being Mr Lazy, doesn't get up in the morning like you and I do.

He gets up in the afternoon!

And little Miss Late, being little Miss Late, is always late for work.

So she doesn't arrive for work in the morning.

She arrives in the afternoon!

And.

Mr Lazy, being Mr Lazy, doesn't have lunch at lunchtime like you and I do.

He has lunch at suppertime!

And so you see it all works very well.

Very well indeed!

Last Friday evening the telephone rang in Earlybird Cottage.

Little Miss Late had just arrived home from work.

It was Mr Silly on the telephone.

"I've been given some tickets for a dance tomorrow night," he said.

"Would you like to come?"

"Oo, yes please," said Miss Late eagerly.

"Right," replied Mr Silly.

"I'll pick you up at seven o'clock!"

Last Saturday Mr Silly walked up the path to the front door of Earlybird Cottage.

He knocked.

"Come in," called a voice from upstairs.

Mr Silly went in.

"Make yourself at home," called little Miss Late from upstairs.

"I'll be down in a minute!"